American Robins

Julie Murray

Abdo Kids Junior
is an Imprint of Abdo Kids
abdobooks.com

Abdo
STATE BIRDS
Kids

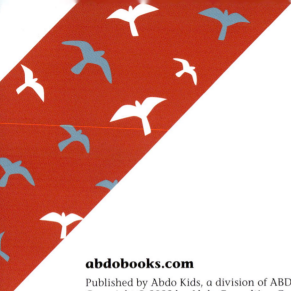

abdobooks.com

Published by Abdo Kids, a division of ABDO, P.O. Box 398166, Minneapolis, Minnesota 55439. Copyright © 2022 by Abdo Consulting Group, Inc. International copyrights reserved in all countries. No part of this book may be reproduced in any form without written permission from the publisher. Abdo Kids Junior™ is a trademark and logo of Abdo Kids.

Printed in the United States of America, North Mankato, Minnesota.

052021

092021

Photo Credits: iStock, Shutterstock

Production Contributors: Teddy Borth, Jennie Forsberg, Grace Hansen

Design Contributors: Candice Keimig, Pakou Moua

Library of Congress Control Number: 2020947586

Publisher's Cataloging-in-Publication Data

Names: Murray, Julie, author.

Title: American robins / by Julie Murray

Description: Minneapolis, Minnesota : Abdo Kids, 2022 | Series: State birds | Includes online resources and index.

Identifiers: ISBN 9781098207137 (lib. bdg.) | ISBN 9781098207977 (ebook) | ISBN 9781098208394 (Read-to-Me ebook)

Subjects: LCSH: State birds--Juvenile literature. | Robins--Juvenile literature. | Birds--Behavior--United States--Juvenile literature.

Classification: DDC 598.297--dc23

Table of Contents

American Robins. 4

State Bird. 22

Glossary. 23

Index 24

Abdo Kids Code. 24

American Robins

American robins live across the US.

5

They live in many places.

They are often seen in yards.

Robins like to sing. You can find them by listening for them.

They have gray feathers.

Their chests are orange.

Their beaks are yellow.

They eat with their beaks.

They like worms, insects, and fruit!

They build nests. The nest is made of grass and mud.

They lay eggs in the nest.

The eggs are blue.

The **chicks hatch** in 2 weeks.

Soon they will fly.

State Bird

WI
Wisconsin

MI
Michigan

CT
Connecticut

Glossary

chick
a bird that has just hatched or a young bird.

hatch
to come out of an egg.

23

Index

beak 12

chest 10

chicks 20

color 10, 12, 18

eggs 18, 20

feathers 10

food 14

habitat 6

nest 16, 18

singing 8

United States 4

Visit **abdokids.com** to access crafts, games, videos, and more!

Use Abdo Kids code **SAK7137** or scan this QR code!